I0746419

BACK IN THE SADDLE

LORELEI JAMES

Back In The Saddle

A Rough Riders Novella
Copyright © 2023 LJLA, LLC, All Rights Reserved.

Ridgeview Publishing
April 2023 Print Edition

ISBN: 978-1-941869-17-8

Visit www.loreleijames.com

Cover Design by: Meredith Blair
Cover Photo by: photo.ua/Bigstock.com/112867757
Edited by: Lindsey Faber
Interior Designed and Formatted by: BB eBooks Co., Ltd. –
www.bbebooksthailand.com

Rough Riders Series

(in reading order)

Long Hard Ride
Rode Hard
Cowgirl Up and Ride
Tied Up, Tied Down
Rough, Raw and Ready
Branded As Trouble
Strong, Silent Type (novella)
Shoulda Been A Cowboy
All Jacked Up
Raising Kane
Slow Ride (short story)
Cowgirls Don't Cry
Chasin' Eight
Cowboy Casanova
Kissin' Tell
Gone Country
Short Rides (novella anthology)
Redneck Romeo
Cowboy Take Me Away
Long Time Gone (novella)
Silver Tongued Devil (Prequel)
Cowboy Bites: A Rough Riders Cookbook

You wanted it, you got it! Thanks to all the readers who participated in the online poll and overwhelmingly picked Cord and AJ for this new short story!

Timeline for *Back in the Saddle*, a Cord and AJ short story; this takes place right before *Redneck Romeo*, around the same time Dalton McKay returns to Wyoming.

I T WAS OFFICIAL: her marriage had officially gone to the dogs.

Every day this week—heck, every day the past few months—Cord hadn't kissed her goodbye.

AJ had been hopeful for a smooch this morning upon hearing him re-enter the house. She'd propped herself provocatively in the doorway between the entryway and the kitchen, watching as he strode right past her to snatch the keyring he'd left on the bench. Cord hadn't spared her a second glance, but he had reached down to scratch the dog's head before hustling out the door.

What happened after that…not her proudest moment, but she *had* been hopping mad.

She eyed their blue heeler, Chichi, who wore a suspiciously smug look. "If your master keeps that up, he'll be bunking in the barn with you."

Chichi cocked her head.

"Piece of advice, pooch. Wagging your behind at him is a bust as far as getting his attention. Trust me. I've already tried it." She sighed. "Has it really come to this? I'm confiding my marital woes to the dog."

Her annoyance probably didn't qualify as a real marital issue to anyone else. But it bugged the crap out of her since this weird disconnect with Cord had been dragging on forever. At first she'd chalked up his distraction to the demands of calving season. But that season had come and gone, yet as this *no kissy, no huggy* situation lingered, AJ worried it'd become their new normal. Or worse yet, Cord was utterly clueless that his daily show of affection toward her had dwindled to zero.

The first time she'd brought it up, Cord's defensiveness had kicked in and he'd lit into her about all of his responsibilities. The second time she'd mentioned it, Cord opted for sarcasm. AJ suspected if she brought it up again, he'd sigh, mutter *sorry darlin'* and offer a perfunctory peck on the cheek each morning in a half-assed attempt at placating her.

No thank you.

"Mama?"

She blinked and glanced down at her youngest son, Vaughn. "Yes, sweetie?"

"Why're you sad?"

AJ ruffled his blond curls—he was the only one of their children who had inherited her hair color. "It's nothing for you to worry about."

"Are you missin' sissy?"

Avery, her only girl child, and the closest one in age to Vaughn, had recently started all-day kindergarten, much to Vaughn's dismay. "I'm missing something," she murmured. Then she smoothed the hair she'd tousled. "Are you ready to head into town?"

"Yep. Got my backpack."

She smiled at the massive camo backpack, stuffed to the gills with god only knew what a four-year old needed for six hours away from home. "You've jammed a lot of stuff in there, pard. You sure you don't need me to carry it?"

Vaughn scoffed, his expression so like Cord's that her heart squeezed. "I'm not a *baby*, mama."

"My mistake. Go get your boots on and I'll be right there."

With only one kiddo in her eight passenger Suburban, the too-quiet drive from the ranch into Sundance gave AJ too much time to think.

Even when she understood it wasn't fair to compare their past to their present, she couldn't stop her thoughts from focusing on the hungry way Cord used to look at her. Those work-roughened hands all over her all the time. The sexual tension between them that needed an immediate release.

This wasn't about sex, except recently that was the only time Cord showed affection. In the moment their bodies connected, his blue eyes filled with a heart-stopping mix of love, desire and satisfaction. A look that hadn't faltered over the years, a look that belonged to her alone.

God. Maybe she oughta quit fretting over what she missed and be thankful for what she had.

Yet…what if she was at fault? She couldn't stand the thought of this disconnect continuing much longer.

After dropping Vaughn off at the community center for preschool, she headed down the street and parked in her spot behind the Sandstone Building. Juggling her messenger bag, Diet Pepsi and keys, she unlocked the back door, stepping into the cool darkness. The ever-present scents of essential oils filled her nose and she breathed in a deep, calming breath. This space was her sanctuary.

While she loved being home on the ranch with Cord and their kids, she'd continued to run Healing Touch, the massage studio she'd opened the first year of their marriage.

After the birth of Beau, baby boy number two, AJ leased out part of her space to another massage therapist. Dante Blackstone, a Casper transplant, specialized in rehabilitation massage therapy. He worked two days a week on location and the other days in the studio. While they usually alternated days, sometimes their schedules meshed, and they'd be in the office together. AJ expelled a sigh of relief Dante wasn't around. She'd be tempted to blurt out all her frustrations and fears because confiding in the dog had gotten her nowhere.

Striving to put her worries out of her mind, she popped in her earbuds and cranked the music as she cleaned and restocked her space. Then her ten o'clock cancelled, leaving her at loose ends for an hour. Even online retail therapy hadn't brightened her mood.

Promptly at ten-fifty-seven, Ainsley Hamilton sailed in for her eleven o'clock appointment. As usual, the bank president was smartly dressed: a cream-colored silk blouse and a royal blue A-line skirt that mirrored the stripes in the blue plaid suit jacket. Gray open-toed pumps and matching handbag completed the ensemble.

AJ whistled. "Lookin' good today, Lady A."

Ainsley blushed. "Thanks. Big meeting this morning and Ben is taking me to lunch."

"He's coming into town just for lunch with you?" Ainsley's husband Ben McKay and his older brother,

Quinn, ran the northern most section of the massive McKay Ranch and were Cord's cousins.

"You sound surprised."

"I am. I don't know that Cord has ever specifically met *me* for lunch."

"Ever?" Ainsley asked with genuine shock.

"Well, not since we were first married. If we have to take the kids to an appointment or something during the week, we might stop for a bite before we head back to the ranch."

"Don't take this the wrong way, but that sucks. Especially since I doubt you two ever get to enjoy a quiet meal alone at home."

*With all those kids…*went unsaid.

Then Ainsley backtracked. "But I'm sure it's fine if it works for you."

"I'm beginning to wonder if it isn't broken," AJ muttered. But she knew Ainsley had heard her when her eyes narrowed. AJ offered a quick smile. "Never mind. Hit the dressing room and I'll meet you back there."

Ainsley sauntered to the door off to the left. The dressing room had a rear passthrough that allowed the client to enter the treatment room without having to backtrack through the reception area.

AJ washed her hands and selected the eucalyptus

oil Ainsley preferred. For background noise she chose instrumental music with soft chimes layered over gentle guitar chords.

Ainsley emerged and dropped her robe before she hopped up on the table. She stretched out on her belly, her arms above her head. Her casual approach to nudity had actually shocked AJ; she'd expected the bank president to be modest. Ainsley had noticed her shock and had laughed. "In my life BB—Before Ben— being naked in any situation made me burn with shame. My husband has…reformed that attitude and now I'm practically a nudist." That admission had forged an honest friendship between them and AJ looked forward to their sessions.

"Am I working on your shoulders today?" she asked.

"Yes, please. And if there's time, can you check out my right calf? I've had weird cramps there the past week."

"No problem. What level do you need today?"

"Medium hard? Gentler on my arms."

"All right. Now inhale. Let go of all the tension you're holding. Exhale slowly. Good. Twice more." She didn't put her hands on Ainsley until her last drawn-out exhale.

Some clients were chatty during their treatment.

Some only spoke to ask for pressure adjustment. Ainsley fell somewhere in between. During the most intense portion of the tissue work, she concentrated on breathing and keeping her shoulders relaxed. But when AJ drifted to her lower back, she tuned in and made small talk. Ainsley surprised AJ when she said, "Is everything all right with you and Cord?"

"Eh. It's the same old same old with Cord."

"And is that part of the problem?" When AJ didn't immediately respond, Ainsley added, "Look, I know you're close to your sisters-in-law, and maybe you've mentioned whatever is going on with you and Cord to them, but it seems you need to talk to someone now. I'm here and it's not like I'll blab far and wide about it."

AJ snorted. "Here's where you'll remind me that you're a banker used to keeping everyone in town's secrets."

"Here's where I remind you that we are family, but mostly I'll remind you that I was married before Ben. I know what it's like to question what you're willing to live with or live without in a relationship."

When AJ's hands quit moving, Ainsley lifted her head and looked over her shoulder. "Or am I wrong?"

"That's the thing; I don't know *what's* wrong. In the past few months, Cord has stopped being the affectionate man I fell in love with. I mean, we still have sex. I get off, he gets off. But outside of the bedroom? No ass-grabbing, no playful swats, no handholding, no reaching over to squeeze my leg as we're driving. No crowding me and kissing my neck when I cook or sliding me onto his lap when we watch TV. I can't remember the last time he purposely sought me out and kissed me goodbye before we started our days. And unless we go to bed at the exact same time, he doesn't bother telling me goodnight. Maybe it sounds trivial, but I've gotten used to constant affection from him. And poof, it's suddenly gone."

"That is odd. His memory isn't failing?"

"No more selective male memory than usual."

"Have you tried tracking him down to kiss him before you leave?"

"Once." AJ dug her thumbs into Ainsley's thick calf muscle. "I followed him out to his truck but before I could put a liplock on him, he said he did not have time to add another task to his to do list. So when I fantasized about putting him in a *headlock*, I retreated like a dog with its tail between its legs." She groaned. "I know he's dealing with a million things, but I didn't deserve to be dismissed."

"What did he say?" Ainsley asked.

AJ imitated Cord. "Christ, AJ, don't you think I got enough shit to worry about without you addin' to it?

I'm sorry I haven't been playin' grab-ass with you in the barn and sucking face with you in the kitchen, but it ain't like I'm ignorin' you. I'm right here with you, every damn day, doin' the best I can. What else do you want from me?"

Ainsley laughed. "You do a pretty good Cord imitation. But would he really say that?"

"Well, it was more like he barked it at me, which is ironic, since the damn dog gets more petting and stroking than I do." She blew out a breath. "You probably think I'm ridiculous."

"I think you're frustrated."

"Mostly I'm scared if I do cowgirl up and demand he hear me out, that I'll freeze and forget what I wanted to say or turn into a madwoman who yells and throws things."

A beat passed and Ainsley said, "Maybe if you practice talking to him like you were giving a speech, you'll find the right phrasing. Or at least avoid the words that'll cause him to clam up or get defensive. I still have to do that before dealing with touchy subjects with Ben."

AJ gentled her kneading thumbs as she considered Ainsley's suggestion. "Prepare a speech? That seems weird. Then again, I'm out of ideas."

"Just try it. What would you do if Cord walked in

right now and heard us discussing this?"

A multitude of answers scrolled through her head. Blush? Laugh it off? Apologize?

No. She'd backtalk. Get him riled up. Because then she'd be his total focus and he'd *have* to listen to her.

"AJ?"

For a moment she imagined it *was* Cord's voice, that little snap in his tone when he impatiently said her name. "Hold it right there, McKay. Wipe that angry bull look off your face. I'm not trash-talking you; I'm talking to a friend about what's bugging *me*. Be glad Keely isn't my confidante. Her advice begins and ends with slipping you Viagra because you've always been a grumpy old fucker."

Ainsley snickered but AJ kept delivering a smackdown to the phantom Cord. "This isn't about sex. It's about intimacy. And affection. I'm worried you haven't realized there *is* a gulf growing between us. When I've brought it up, you claim you're doing the best you can. But that's not true. I've had your best for years and honey, this ain't it."

After a brief pause, Ainsley said, "That sounded perfectly on point to me. Now you just need to tell the person who needs to hear it."

"Yeah. I'll fit that conversation in when we get a moment alone. Oh, right. That's almost never."

A muffled noise caught her attention. Where had that come from? She didn't have another client scheduled for an hour. "Go ahead and get dressed. I'll meet you out front."

AJ glanced around the reception area. No sign of a delivery. Didn't look like Dante had popped by.

Then she noticed that the dressing room door was wide open.

Ainsley probably hadn't gotten the door completely closed earlier. When the heater kicked on, the door blew open. That's probably all she'd heard.

CORD HUSTLED BACK to his truck, his heart thudding as fast as his booted feet.

Inside the vehicle, he curled his hands around the steering wheel and closed his eyes.

What the ever-lovin' fuck?

After AJ had acted completely out of character this morning, he decided to check on her, so he'd come to town.

Rather than slipping in the back door as he usually did, he'd entered the studio through the front, intending to catch her between clients. He planned to scroll through farm and ranch reports on his phone while he waited, when he'd heard—"Eh. It's the same old, same old with Cord"—not uttered in that loving tone his wife normally used.

Curiosity had gotten the better of him; an open dressing room door was an open invitation. And man, had he gotten an earful, standing close enough to hear every blasted word about his failings and missteps.

He'd almost panicked when he'd heard "Hold it right there, McKay" thinking AJ had busted him, but she'd kept up her rant and he'd listened until Ainsley had given AJ props for her practiced speech.

Then he'd beat feet outta there.

While Cord didn't dismiss her concerns, feelings, whatever, it was a load of horseshit that he'd been that inattentive to her for as long as she claimed.

You sure about that, McKay?

He snorted at AJ's assertation that he never took her to lunch. Maybe he hadn't done it in a while, but he had grabbed food and shared it with her at her studio.

Not the same thing, buddy. Dropping off a burger because you were in town getting tractor parts is not the same as setting up a time specifically for a meal with only her.

Okay, that was a valid point. It'd been longer than he cared to admit since he'd put effort into carving out alone time for them. Granted, it'd become harder with each new kid they added to their family, but AJ hadn't expressed disappointment to Ainsley that they hadn't gone on date nights or taken a couples' weekend; her complaint centered on his inattention to her even when they were in the *same* room.

Christ. There wasn't any doubt he'd been moody and exhausted since they'd started haying. And maybe sharper in tone than usual in his responses.

But his recall of the day she'd chased him to his truck played out a bit differently in his mind. No denying he'd barked at her, but the woman hadn't taken into account that he'd hauled his ass outta bed at four a.m. so Ky could help with the morning cattle check before he raced to town for his first football practice of the day. He'd come home to refill his thermos after he'd gotten a text from Colt that he wouldn't be on hand, which left Cord working by himself. Again.

So yeah, he'd been pissed off and overwhelmed before she added to it by complaining he hadn't been his usual horny self. Or that's how he'd taken it.

Appeared he'd taken it wrong.

Thinking back to the day a week or so later, when AJ had sauntered into the barn and remarked his horse got more daily affection than she did…apparently his crack about riding her until she got all sweaty and finishing her off with a rubdown and a sugar cube hadn't been as funny to her as it had been to him.

How had they gotten so out of synch? From the moment they'd gotten together, AJ had been an open book. She hadn't played games. She tackled problems with a mix of fortitude, love and good cheer and wasn't shy about sharing her opinions. That's why he loved her; she called him on his shit rather than putting up with it. What didn't make sense was that she'd turned this "he said/she said" miscommunication into a serious threat to their relationship. It was just a little hiccup.

They needed to get back on track. And sooner rather than later.

Cord scrubbed his hands over his razor-stubbled face. Alone time. Right. First things first ditching the kids for a night.

He called Keely.

"Hey big bro. What's up?"

"I need a favor. Can you pick Vaughn up from preschool when you get the twins?"

"Sure. Is that all you need?"

Cord blew out a breath. "I don't know. I'm tryin' to surprise my wife with a date night—a kid-free overnight date night—and I'm not sure how to make that happen. We McKays each have too many kids to dump the lot of them off with one family. And I don't wanna spring this on Mom and Dad last minute."

"Well, I can pick up both Vaughn and Avery and keep them until noon tomorrow. Maybe Colby and Channing could take Foster and Beau? They'd probably prefer to be with their boy cousin gang."

"Good idea. I'll call him."

"Is this nookie-fest happening after Kyler's football game tonight?"

Crap. He'd known Kyler had plans, but in his relief that he'd had one less kid to worry about shuffling off, he'd forgotten *why* Ky wouldn't be home. "Um, we're skipping tonight's game."

Keely gasped. "*You*? Skipping out on Kyler's game? You *never* do that."

Wrong. He'd missed games when ranch business took priority, so Miss-Know-it-all didn't know everything. "Do I need to pack some stuff for the kids and drop it off?"

"Nope. I got you covered."

"One other thing, don't talk to AJ. I am tryin' to keep it a surprise."

"I won't. I'll text you when I'm home with the kiddos."

"Thanks, K. I mean it."

Next he called his brother Colby's cell, but he

didn't answer so Cord tried reaching his sister-in-law Channing.

"Did you mean to call me, Cord, or was this another saddle dial?" Channing intoned sweetly.

"Butt dial someone once and they never forget it," he groused. "I tried reaching Colby first, but he didn't pick up."

"He's right here so I can put you on speaker."

Shuffling sounds and murmurs crackled in his ear. "Hey Cord. You checkin' up on me to see if I'm fucking around on my lunch break?"

Cord snorted. "Even if I was, you'd take your time getting back to work just to annoy me. I'm calling because I need a favor."

"Yeah? Should I be worried about this favor you need since you *never* ask for nothin'?"

"Maybe I *don't* ask 'cause you pop off a bunch of smart-ass questions when I do." And it's easier just to handle things myself rather than deal with your excuses, Cord added silently.

Colby sighed. "Yeah, I am kind of a dick. So what's up?"

"Any chance you can pick up Foster and Beau from the bus stop and keep them overnight, until noon tomorrow? I'm tryin' to surprise AJ with a date night."

"Ooh. Romantic," Channing said, "AJ will love

that. There's no problem adding two more McKay boys to the mix of our own. Just call the school and send a message to their classrooms to have them get off at our bus stop."

"Will do. And thanks."

"One last thing before you hang up," Colby said. "You want me to finish mowing that section of ditch you started yesterday?"

He frowned at his phone. "No. I can finish it on Monday. Why?"

"So *you're* done workin' for the day?" he said skeptically.

"Thought I made that clear?"

"What Colby is getting at," Channing interjected, "is if you expect him to return to…umm…ranch stuff this afternoon, or if he can continue to hover over me until it's time to pick up the kids."

Ranch stuff. Lord. Was AJ the only woman in this family who understood what the daily grind of ranching entailed? And maybe, Cord thought bitterly, he'd like the chance to hover over his own wife, because apparently, he hadn't been doing enough of that. "Don't know why the hell you're askin' me. Colby does what he wants, when he wants…or not at all. "Shoot me a text when you've got the boys."

Since Cord was in town, he stopped at the elementary school and signed off in person for the change in afterschool transportation plans for Avery, Foster and Beau. Then he popped into the community center and changed the pickup form for Vaughn.

He'd barely reached the outskirts of town when his phone rang. The caller ID on the truck's display read Kyler. Frowning, he poked the answer button. "Ky? Everything all right?"

"Yeah. Is everything all right with the brat pack? I saw your truck at the school."

Only Cord seemed bothered by Kyler referring to his siblings as the brat pack. "Everything is fine." He paused and said sharply, "How'd you know I was there? Ain't you supposed to be in class?"

"It's lunchtime, Dad. A bunch of us were sitting outside. So what's goin' on? You're never in town during workin' hours."

Another family member ascribing the word *never* to his behavior. Was he really that predictable? "I needed to deal with a few things before I spring a surprise date night on AJ. Your brothers and sister are staying with their cousins. You still crashing with Hayden?"

"Yep, me'n Anton both are. We'll probably hang out after the football game, see if anything is goin' on in town."

"Sorry we'll miss the game tonight."

"Not a big deal. We're playing Belle and they suck so I think coach is gonna mostly rest his starters."

"Have a good game anyway. And don't you boys go out stirring up shit that'll get your uncle Cam hot on your tail."

Kyler laughed. "Anton is a good deterrent. He doesn't wanna piss off his dad either, regardless if he's in his deputy uniform."

"Good. See ya tomorrow afternoon, son."

Cord left the radio off as he drove back to the ranch, trying to come up with a more solid plan than a kid-free night. He didn't want things to play out in the usual pattern—dinner out, home to fuck, then fall asleep. He wanted to specifically address her "the man he used to be" remark without any of this beating-around-the-bush bullshit.

Beating around the bush.

Huh.

He could work with that.

He cracked a huge grin. Oh, this was gonna be some fun.

AJ'S PHONE RANG two minutes before her last appointment started. Normally she wouldn't have answered it, but Cord was calling. And he never called her when she was working.

"Cord? What's wrong?"

He chuckled. "Are my phone calls rare enough that you assume something bad has happened?"

"Maybe. Anyway, what's up?"

"You've got the day off from bein' a taxi service. I'll handle the kids today. You just come on home when you're done workin'."

Her forehead wrinkled with confusion. "You mean all the kids except Vaughn? I still need to get him since I'm in town?"

"Nope. Gotcha covered."

"Are you sure? Because—"

"Just because you usually do all this stuff doesn't mean I don't know how to do it and can't step in once in a while."

"But…I don't understand."

"I know you don't, but you will." A pause. "And for the record, baby doll? That's one."

The growly, sexy tone she hadn't heard in a long time sent a shiver down her spine.

"Cord?"

Silence. He'd hung up.

Damn man.

Then Marguerite hobbled in, and AJ had no choice but to focus on her client.

An hour later she locked up for the weekend. She wondered if she should swing by the grocery store and grab something quick for supper. Then she remembered Ky had a football game, and the kids would expect to load up on concession-stand junk, so she was off the hook for tonight's meal.

AJ barely registered the drive home. She parked on the concrete pad in front of the garage, next to Cord's truck. She'd cleared the first two steps when she noticed Cord lounging in the chair next to the porch swing.

She swallowed her disappointment that he hadn't leapt up to welcome her home with a hug and a kiss. Then she noticed he'd stretched out his long denim-clad legs and propped his bare feet on the log railing. A lowball glass rested on the table next to him. He wore a white T-shirt that hugged his broad chest, highlighting the work-honed muscles in his arms, and the slope of his belly. Good Lord the man was fine. "You look comfy."

"I am." He tipped his head to the chair opposite him. "Have a seat and I'll pour ya a happy hour special."

She tried not to show shock at his playful response.

When was the last time she'd seen him this relaxed? Dropping into the chair, she sighed. "It's gonna be a beautiful night."

"Yes, it is." Cord handed her a glass three quarters full of amber liquid with a large ice cube bobbing in the center.

"What's this happy hour special?"

"Crown apple."

Her favorite. She smiled and held her glass up for a toast. "TGIF."

He touched his glass to hers.

After the first sip warmed her throat, she basked in the last rays of sunshine and the quiet.

Wait. It was *too* quiet. "Where are the kids? Watching movies or something?"

"Nope. Avery and Vaughn are havin' a sleepover at Keely's. Foster and Beau are stayin' with Colby. Ky is crashing with Hayden after the game. So we're all alone."

AJ's mouth dropped open. "That's…"

"Surprising?" he supplied.

Not the norm for you to make personal plans for us, especially on a Friday night. Cord actually looked forward to Friday night football games with her and the kids. "Cord. What is going on?"

His too-blue gaze locked on hers. "Why don't you

tell me?"

"What's that supposed to mean?" she shot back.

"That. Right there. That's what I'm talkin' about. You've been downright pissy. Anytime I ask what's wrong, you get snippy and snap that everything is *fine*."

She looked away. "Oh yeah? I can't remember the last time you asked me what was wrong."

That shut him up. Briefly. "I don't think your memory is as reliable as you seem to believe."

AJ knocked back another drink. "So what is this? Some kind of anger management intervention?"

"Should it be? 'Cause darlin', you literally threw my lunch at me this morning."

AJ felt a wash of shame again, remembering tearing out of the house after he'd so pointedly ignored her, whipping the soft-sided lunch bag at him and yelling, "Have a nice day, asshole." But she doubled down on her pettiness and retorted, "I'm not sorry."

"I know you're not. Still confused about why you shouted *woof woof* before storming off."

Oh. She'd forgotten about that last dig. "Speaking of…where is your faithful sidekick?"

"Chichi is tucked in for the night. Which is why it's just you and me, workin' through this mad of yours, without interruptions."

Her heart rate spiked with hope.

"It's been too goddamned long since we've been completely alone for more than an hour or two. And I'm truly sorry about that. Goin' forward, I'll pay better mind to it. The kids will be back tomorrow at noon. So the night is ours. The morning too."

AJ stared into her glass as she swirled the last of the whiskey around the ice cube. "What happens next?"

"That, my beautiful wife, is entirely up to you."

She glanced over as Cord dropped a folded piece of fabric on the table, followed by a white sheet of paper. "What's that?"

"Your choices on how we spend our time together." He lifted the blank page. "Option one: you choose. Could be a traditional date night. We get dressed up, have a nice dinner in Deadwood. Maybe do some dancin'. Whatever you want. You call the shots."

"And that option?"

Cord smirked at her and picked up the black bandana, running the folded section between his fingers. "This is a blindfold. You put your blind faith in me and *I* call all the shots."

For a panicked moment, she studied him. Had he somehow gotten wind of her conversation with Ainsley?

No, it'd definitely been the speedball—aka the

lunch—she'd thrown him that'd convinced him to take action.

He dropped his feet to the decking and stood. Then he planted himself in front of her, his hands on the arms of the chair, lowering his upper body until they were face to face. "I'm gonna lobby on my own behalf for you to choose option two." Cord rubbed the smooth part of his upper cheek across hers. "Please."

The scent of him…she closed her eyes. Lime shaving cream. Laundry detergent from his clean T-shirt. Sun-warmed skin. A hint of whiskey. And that heady, underlying musk that was his alone.

Then his lips were at her ear. "I wanna get us back where we need to be, baby doll. Here, in our own house, where we're the most comfortable bein' ourselves." He lightly tugged her earlobe between his teeth until she groaned. "You've got three minutes to decide." He pushed away from her and started for the front door.

"But—"

He paused and sent her a stern look over his shoulder. "That's two."

AJ had forgotten how his little counting game affected her: maddening and enticing.

She hadn't needed the allotted time to make her choice.

Seemed longer than three minutes before she heard his feet shuffling across the decking.

She waved the bandana over her head in surrender.

Had Cord just exhaled a huge sigh of relief?

His hands landed on her shoulders and she jumped.

"Easy," he soothed as his palms glided up her neck. "Just making sure this is tied nice and tight." He adjusted the cloth and fiddled with the knot until he was satisfied.

She heard a soft thud and felt his shoulders brush the insides of her knees. Warm palms squeezed the back of her calves. Cord untied her work boots and slipped them off her feet. Then he removed her socks. His hands traveled up her body to her hips. "Stand."

After helping her up, he said, "Lift your arms."

As soon as she complied, Cord yanked her shirt over her head.

But before she could protest, he'd buried his face in her cleavage while he unhooked her bra. "Christ, I love your tits." Then he performed a quick maneuver that brought her arms down between them, her biceps pushing her breasts together as he used her bra to bind her forearms.

When she wobbled, he placed her fingers just inside the waistband of his jeans. "Hold on."

That's when she realized he'd taken off his shirt too.

"Tilt your head back," he commanded as his teeth grazed her shoulder.

Cord didn't speak. He didn't give her a play-by-play of how he planned to turn her into a quivering mess of need; he'd memorized and perfected that playbook years ago. His mouth knew exactly where to suck, where to lick, how to exploit the secret spots where soft, wet kisses and heated breath turned her spine to jelly.

When he followed the contours of her body with those callused fingertips, AJ whispered, "Unfair," and reveled in the gooseflesh rippling across her skin. With a light touch, his fingers repeatedly followed the same course; up her sides, around her shoulders, pausing at the nape of her neck to trace her spine down to the waistband of her jeans, then slowly up her back, over her traps and down her arms.

AJ's breathing turned choppy as she anticipated each touch. It'd been ages since he'd taken such care in drawing out their foreplay. She went still. She hadn't done the same for him recently either.

Cord paused in his delicious torture. "What made you tense up just now?"

"Guilt," she blurted out. "I haven't touched you like

this, just for the sheer pleasure of it, for a while. And I'm sorry."

"Hey, hey. No guilt allowed. I'm reminding both of us how much I worship this sexy body of yours." Then he kissed her until she melted into him, once again lost in the familiar heat that built between them.

The next time AJ shivered, he stopped. He uncurled her fingers from his waistband and untied her hands. "Let's go inside. It *is* getting a might nipply out here."

Although she couldn't see him, she imagined that wicked grin as he ogled her breasts. "Hilarious, McKay."

He lifted her arms and placed them on his shoulders. "Jump up and wrap your legs around my waist."

"You don't have to carry me inside."

"I *want* to carry you."

AJ almost said, "But what about your back?" thought better of it, and changed it to, "You just want my tits in your face."

"Always, baby doll."

She held on while he meandered into the house, his mouth greedily sucking and his hands kneading her ass. Her back met the wall and the restraint he'd had outside vanished.

His lust-filled growl vibrated against her skin and

shot straight between her legs. After nursing four babies, her nipples hadn't regained full sensation, but she loved how much Cord was still obsessed with her tits, and his hunger fueled her own.

When he paused to drag the hard ridge of his cock across her clit, she ground against him, panting, "How long do I have to wear the blindfold?"

"Until I take it off."

Don't say it.

Cord appeared to be awaiting her complaint. When she remained mum, he said, "I'd expected this sassy mouth to throw out a few more buts, and I'm slightly disappointed I only ended up with two."

"Two what?"

"You'll see."

"Not with this blindfold on I won't."

The man laughed.

Laughed. Damn him.

He stepped back and set her on the floor. "C'mon."

AJ expected he'd take her upstairs to their bedroom, but given the scent of wood smoke, they were in the living room. "You lit a fire?"

"Figured since you were gonna be nekkid for the foreseeable future you might like some extra warmth, but I won't stoke it again if you say the word."

"I like it—not that I can see the crackling flames—I

just thought—"

Cord's mouth came down on hers. He lifted his lips long enough to murmur, "No thinkin' tonight. Now strip outta them jeans. Ditch that black thong too."

Her fingers paused over the zipper. "How'd you know the color of my—"

"If you think I don't pay attention when you're half-dressed in our bedroom, then it's my responsibility to remind you that I do."

Defiantly, AJ raised her chin. "I don't want to be just another damn responsibility you have to see too, Cord."

Framing her face in his hands, he gentled his tone. "Sorry, darlin', I misspoke. I meant to say I notice everything about you, every day, even when you think I don't."

"Oh. Well, okay then."

A quick kiss, then he said, "Jeans off. Now."

Ten seconds later, she said, "There. I'm bare-assed in my living room. You happy?"

"Yep, but that sass is gonna get you in trouble."

"Bring it. I can handle it."

He sighed. "And to think I'd started feelin' guilty about this first part because you were bein' pretty sweet."

"This first part?" she repeated.

"Worried?"

"Nope," she lied.

"Good." He gripped her shoulders. "Take two steps back. Now sit."

Her behind met cold wood. Curved cold wood. She wiggled and the thing squeaked. "Wait. Is this my new saddle stand?"

"Yep."

"You brought my saddle stand *inside* the house?"

"I can't do this in the barn, baby doll; you'd freeze your tits off. And with what we paid for this damn thing, it oughta have multiple uses."

Unbelievable. "Cord! This is for a saddle. It won't hold my weight."

"It will."

"How do you know?"

"Because I caught all four kids sittin' on it last weekend. Reach out and grab the sides. Good. Now widen your knees. Stay just like that."

Her heartrate spiked when she felt rope circle her wrists, then the slight bite of pain as he cinched it by looping the rope across her thighs and under her knees. She jumped when he brushed a kiss on the hollow below her ear.

"I've fantasized about tyin' you to this thing from the moment we dragged it home. You oughta see yourself, trussed up with a red rope, that pink pussy wet for me."

Heat bloomed across her face and chest.

"You're pretty as a picture, darlin'." A pause then, "Smile."

"You better not have taken my picture like this, Cord McKay."

"Or what," he whispered in her other ear. "Don't pretend you don't wanna peek at it and see how damn hot you look."

That gruff voice sent tingles down her neck.

"Don't worry. No one will ever see the only pic in my spank bank."

"That's not the point! How would you like it if I took a picture of your dick?"

He eased the blindfold down just enough to show AJ the twinkle in his blue eyes. "I'd love it. I'd even snap a pic myself and message it to you, but only if you ask nicely because I don't wanna be accused of sending unsolicited dick pics."

AJ couldn't help it. She laughed. His eyes were laughing too before he covered her eyes again.

"Now quit distracting me from meting out your penalties. Only two backtalking buts this time. I think you'll be grateful you held your tongue." Then his hands were on her thighs as he lowered himself to his knees. "But that don't mean I gotta hold mine."

This instant Cord put his mouth on her, she nearly screamed.

Long torturous licks from the bottom of her pussy to the top.

Sneaky soft nibbles on the flesh surrounding her clit that were there and gone.

Hard sucks on the insides of her thighs.

Hands stroking her calves.

Fingers dancing up her shins.

Palms enclosing her knees.

Breath drifting over her sensitive tissues every time he changed position.

AJ surrendered to him. Loving and hating how expertly he played with her. She'd forgotten how masking her sight had increased the potency of her other senses.

Cord finally did that swirly tongue thing around her clit, and she automatically arched back, forgetting for a moment where she was.

The saddle stand rocked, and the ropes tightened.

He righted her before she tipped over, murmuring, "Easy."

"Cord. I can't stay still."

"Try," he said, stopping that fantastically flicking tongue as he pushed a finger inside her. "Makes my dick hard that you're dripping wet for me." He added another finger.

Her response morphed into a low wail as he suctioned his lips around her clit while he stroked her G-spot.

That tingling, pulling sensation started to gather steam. Her legs were shaking and she was seconds away from throbbing orgasmic bliss, when Cord stopped.

"No, don't stop! I'm so close."

"I know." He nuzzled her mound, then placed a kiss above her clit before he backed away.

Where did he think he was going?

"Cord?"

His breath tickled her ear and she jumped. "One down. One to go."

"One what?" she panted. She was teetering on that knife's edge of madness. Her sex was swollen and pulsing, and she'd beg for release if she had to.

"One penalty down, one to go."

Somehow those words permeated her lust-addled brain. "This is my penalty? You build me up and up and then...*deny* me the orgasm?"

"Holdin' you off will make the orgasm more intense." His mouth followed the straining arch of her neck. "I could spend all goddamned night gorging myself on your delicious cunt," he said in the deep growly tone that made her shudder from head to toe.

Except this time, all it did was make her mad. "You're not serious about keeping me on the edge like this."

"Oh, I assure you, baby doll, I'm very serious about it."

"You bastard!"

The man had the audacity to chuckle. "Wanna take a break before I start round two?" She heard him rustling around on the sofa. "I picked up a pizza for supper. Want me to throw it in the oven?"

"I don't want any fucking pizza! I want to come!"

Cord didn't say anything. Then he sighed dramatically. "Fine. No break it is."

"Cord. You can't do that again. It's not—"

He took her mouth in a hard kiss. He tasted of her. Of them. Instead of increasing her frustration, it settled her down.

Just as he knew it would.

"Here's a quick history lesson, since you seemed to've forgotten." Another hungry kiss only increased her unfulfilled ache. "You agreed that any backtalk from you usin' the word *but* when we were discussing important things, gave me the right to administer whatever penalty I deemed fit. Since you've been withholding your feelings to the point you're throwin' stuff at me…well, this penalty couldn't be any more perfect."

"Does that mean you're ready to talk about things without getting all pissy with me?"

A sweet kiss softened the hard set of her mouth. "Oh, we'll talk. Guaranteed. But it ain't gonna happen when I have my feisty wife completely trussed up and at my mercy."

"Cord, I'm—"

"AJ. You know that I'd never do anything to hurt you."

"But I'm hurting now," she said in her most repentant tone.

His palms made another leisurely pass over her chest. "Then it's a lucky thing I gotta redo the ropes."

"That's not what I meant!"

"Then maybe you oughta say exactly what you mean."

The pressure across her thighs eased. He maneuvered her onto her back while her hands remained bound to the saddle stand, which was now above her head.

He pushed her legs apart, stretching out beside her, his bare hip against her thigh.

"Comfortable?" she bit out.

"Getting there."

Silence.

"Are you just staring at me?"

"Yep."

"Why?"

"Because lately all we've made time for is a fast fuck in the dark. So when I've got the time to admire this body, I'm gonna do so." He traced her jawline with the back of his hand. "You're especially beautiful in the firelight."

Why did the man have to be so sweet before he tortured her?

He planted a firm kiss on the upper swell of her left breast.

Then, "Ah, here it is."

"What?" escaped a second before she heard the buzz.

No. He wouldn't.

But he did. Of course he did.

He circled her left nipple with the tip of her vibrator.

She nearly shot out of her skin because they'd never played around with it *there* before.

And suddenly that spot wasn't as numb as she'd believed.

Damn him and his evil little chuckle.

He delivered such sweet torment, sucking on one nipple while using the vibrator on the other and then switching, so the wetness increased the sensitivity of the vibrations.

When she started to squirm, Cord arced the vibrating tip across her belly.

Her muscles tensed and her skin rippled with goosebumps.

She noticed his breathing had grown harsher with each downward arc toward her gleaming sex. It occurred to her that not only was he denying her pleasure, he wasn't getting any relief either. Which was a change from the other times he'd dealt out penalties—they'd mostly benefited him.

"You bored?"

Startled by his voice so close to her ear, she jumped. "No. Why?"

"Seemed like you zoned out."

A snort escaped. "Like that'd be possible."

He nuzzled the curve of her breast. Then moved the vibrator up to draw lazy circles around each breast.

But what if it *was* possible to act zoned out? She could reverse fake an orgasm. She'd remain still when she felt the orgasm start, just silently enjoying every throbbing pulse, then at the very end, she'd thrash around and pretend like she was *about* to go off. She allowed her lips to curve up just a little; she'd show him.

It was a great plan—a brilliant one, and she'd been full of self-congratulations for outsmarting her husband, when he nestled the vibrator between her pussy lips, like a hotdog in a bun. The entire length vibrated on high from her clit allllllll the way down to the pucker of her ass.

AJ's hips bucked so violently she dislodged the vibrator.

Cord swore and trapped her restless pelvis down with one hand. "You'd rather I did this?"

What had she been thinking? There was no way she could remain still, for christsake, when he did that drawing-tight-circles-around-her-clit thing with the pointed vibrating tip. "Oh yes. Just like that. Don't. Stop."

"Stop thinkin' you can hold back, because I know how fast this thing gets you off, Amy Jo."

"Then quit moving it!"

"Leave it here?" He slid it over her clit, then angled it down and pushed it inside her. "Or here?"

She groaned, "You teasing bastard."

"Yep." And Cord continued to pull it out, tease her clit mercilessly and then push it back inside her. Over and over.

She thrashed and called him names.

Like before, she was one clit twitch away from screaming her release, when the vibrations ended. "Noooooo!" Panting and furious, she opened her mouth and screamed her frustration anyway.

When she finished, Cord said, "I didn't catch that, sweetheart. Did you say something?"

"I said I hate you."

He caressed her thigh. "No, you don't. You're just a little mad."

"No, I'm *big* mad at you, McKay. I'm so horny I think I might die."

"You'll probably scream twice as loud as you just did when I finally fuck you."

"Hah! Wrong-o, bucko. I'm *never* having sex with you again."

That brought out his deep bark of laughter. "Hold still."

He made quick work of untying her arms and helped her sit up. Then he cradled her face in his hands, his thumbs gently stroking her cheekbones.

AJ let his touch soothe her.

She thought he'd been stroking her hair, but he'd unknotted the blindfold.

She blinked at him. Stupidly good-looking man. Yeah that *never having sex with you again* had been an empty threat.

He pressed her hand to his cheek. "Anything you need—besides an orgasm?"

"I'm thirsty."

After another lingering caress, he stood.

Whoa. Cord was completely naked. And completely hard.

"Water or whiskey?"

"Both."

"What about pizza?"

She scowled at him. "I already told you I don't want any goddamned pizza."

"All right. But when I get back, we're gonna talk about why you believe I'm not the affectionate man you married."

Her jaw nearly hit the rug. "You…how did you know?"

"Got quite the earful when I tried to surprise you for lunch today."

"Omigod that noise I heard out front was *you*? Listening in?"

"I couldn't help what I overheard."

She groaned and buried her face in her hands.

"Hope you had time to prepare that speech, cause I promise you'll have my full attention when you deliver it."

CORD RETRIEVED THE happy hour tray from the porch. He'd forgotten about being nekkid, until he returned to the living room and saw his bobbing dick in the dining room mirror.

"If I didn't like that dick so much I might be tempted to punch it," AJ drawled. She watched him approach with those wary silver eyes.

Cord set the tray down on the floor. He added three pieces of split wood to the fire and snagged a pillow off the couch.

AJ had already drained the glass of water and poured them both two shots of whiskey. She'd also wrapped the fleece from the couch around herself.

He reached for the other blanket and settled it across his lap. They faced each other, but his wife's gaze remained riveted on the ice cube in her glass.

After a big swallow of whiskey, he said, "AJ. I was kiddin' about you giving me a speech. I heard everything I needed to earlier today."

"Are you mad?"

When he paused too long, she finally met his gaze. "No, baby doll, I'm not mad. You've got friends, you're gonna talk to them. But I *am* confused. Not about me bein' an ass when you tried to talk to me, there's no disputing that. I'm talkin' about when you said I stopped showing you any affection and it'd been goin' on for months."

"It has been. That's the problem. You *haven't* noticed."

"When did all of this start?"

"During calving season."

Cord raised an eyebrow. "It's been goin' on since February?"

AJ frowned. "Maybe the end of calving."

"So April? When we went to Billings for Easter?"

"No. Things were fine then. Must've been around branding or when school got out."

"We brand the first weekend in May. Kids got out of school at the end of May. So can you narrow it down?"

"I know things started to change after…well, it had something to do with cows or ranch stuff."

And he'd been so confident his wife wouldn't ever utter *ranch stuff*. "Like when we turned the bulls out the end of June?"

"No. I remember it being hotter."

"So during haying? Which started mid-July?"

"That's gotta be it." Her eyes narrowed. "Hey. What's up with the twenty questions? Are you denying you've been distant?"

"I'll admit to bein' distant *recently*, but you've gotta admit this disconnect hasn't been going on forever, or months and months, like you told Ainsley. Baby doll, it's only been six *weeks*."

"What? No. It's been way longer than that."

"Maybe it's seemed longer, but I promise you, it's only been six weeks." He held up his hand to forestall her argument. "I know that, because the last six weeks have been a goddamned blur since both Colby and Colt decided to take family vacations, leaving me to figure out how to get everything done. I'm up at four a.m. which means I'm ready for bed after supper. Hard for me to watch TV with you when I'm asleep. We haven't held hands because we've always got the kids with us and between the two of us, we only have enough hands to hold onto *them*. And no offense, but it's too damn stuffy in the kitchen in the summertime to steal kisses over a hot stove."

She took another drink. "That's what you meant when you said my memory wasn't as reliable as I believed."

He nodded. "But you were also completely on target when you said my distraction has been goin' on since calving. This year it seems the more I do, the easier it is for others to slack off because they know I don't leave stuff undone. And by others, I don't mean

Ky. Don't know what I would've done if he hadn't been around to help me out this summer." Cord glanced down into the glass in his hand. "Before you ask, I haven't said anything to my brothers. Doesn't mean I won't, I'm just—"

"Hoping that things will sort themselves out so you don't have to confront them?" AJ interjected softly.

"Yeah. So darlin', when I heard you talkin' today, I understood why you hesitated in bringing up your frustrations with me. I've done the same damn thing with Colby and Colt. I really hate that you're the one who's suffered from me letting that situation slide."

"And I really hate that you were so exhausted that you couldn't even talk to me about all you were doing trying to hold everything together."

The tears in her eyes hit him as hard as a hoof to the belly. "Darlin', come here."

She fit her body into his, finding the spaces that were empty until she filled them.

Cord rubbed his cheek across the top of her sweat-dampened head, releasing the berry scent of her shampoo and breathing her in.

"Will it be enough if I tell you I'm sorry?" he murmured into her hair.

"Yes." She absentmindedly stroked his chest hair. "But maybe we oughta have a code word to indicate when we need to talk about serious issues."

"Only if the word is blowjob. Cause darlin', I promise every time you say blowjob, I pay close attention."

She elbowed him. "I'm being serious."

"So am I."

"You're pushing your luck, McKay."

Cord rolled them closer to the fireplace, keeping her beneath him. After tenderly pushing her hair off her face, he said, "Am I still pushin' my luck?"

"Only if you deny me an orgasm." She stared back at him. "Cord, did that have a point?"

"Mmm-mmm." He nuzzled her throat. "You thought I'd been withholding affection from you. So I wanted to show you what withholding something really felt like."

"Then you'd act generous and finally allow me to come?"

"Ah ah ah. *You're* the one who claimed your frustration with me wasn't about sex." He teased the edge of her jaw with his teeth. "So I had my hands all over you, just bein' affectionate, touching you in that intimate way that had nothin' to do with sex."

"I don't think your definition and my definition of intimate are the same."

He lifted his head and focused intently on her eyes. "And that, baby doll, was the point."

AJ's face softened. "Point taken, cowboy."

"Good." He rested his forehead against hers. "I love you."

"I love you too." She coasted her fingers down his back with such a light touch his skin broke out in gooseflesh. Then she slapped his ass cheeks. Hard.

"Feel better?"

"I'm waiting for you to make me feel better." She widened her legs and arched her pelvis.

He eased inside her, watching her face. As many times as he'd made love to this woman, he never tired of that dreamy expression clouding her eyes. He still listened for the quick hitch in her breathing and groan of satisfaction as he filled her completely. He whispered, "Slow or fast?"

"Slow."

The firelight flickered over their bodies in motion. And he built the rhythm that reminded them both, at least in this, they were always in perfect synch.

CORD AND AJ were snuggled up in front of the dwindling fire. It'd cooled off in the past hour and he really oughta get up and restoke the fire…but that'd be too much trouble.

Suddenly AJ shivered and threw back the blanket. She hopped up and grabbed her glass of whiskey, knocking back the remainder. Then she stepped over him.

"Where you goin'?"

She sent him a saucy look over her shoulder. "To the hot tub because I'm cold."

"Wait. I need—"

"Some extra recovery time?" she asked sweetly.

"Like hell." Cord threw off the blanket so she could see his cock rising to the challenge.

"Then come on. And bring the bottle."

She sashayed away, not bothering to look back to see if he'd follow, because she knew he would.

GROANING AT THE unnaturally bright shaft of light, Cord untangled their entwined limbs and rolled closer to the nightstand, squinting at the clock.

Jesus. Was it really ten a.m.?

"No, don't get up," AJ complained, scooting her body closer to his.

"Sorry, baby doll. The kids'll be here pretty soon, and we left a helluva mess downstairs." Cord swung around and dropped his feet to the floor. He ran a hand through his hair. "Guess we'll have to skip the romantic horseback ride I'd planned for this morning."

AJ snorted.

He turned and looked at her. "What?"

"Did you really think I'd be eager to have a horse between my legs after you rode me four times last night?"

"Hey, that last time was *your* idea," he retorted with a grin. "Not that I'm complaining."

"I am. Lord. My ass is sore." She yawned. "And I'm hungry." She held up her hand. "Don't suggest pizza; we ate it all, remember?"

His thoughts were a bit muddled about what time AJ had brought the pizza into their bed, he'd definitely remembered devouring it and then devouring her. "We could hit the Tasty Place in Hulett before the kids get back."

"Excellent idea. But I need to shower first. Pretty sure I reek of sex."

Cord rolled back onto the bed and pinned her beneath him. "I love it when you look all mussed up and well-fucked. I especially love how my beard smells after I've had it all over your pussy all night."

"And I've got the beard burns on my thighs to back up that dirty comment." She sifted her fingers through his hair. "Thanks for last night. We needed it."

"We sure did." He kissed her. "And remember any time you want my full attention, just whisper blowjob."

She rolled her eyes. "I guarantee if you don't talk to your brothers and your cousins *this week* about them pulling their weight on this ranch, I will yell blowjob at the top of my lungs until you take care of it. You cannot keep doin' this on your own, Cord. It's affected your health and our family life."

"I know. I will. I promise." Another kiss. "Come on. Let's get dressed and go."

WHEN THEY RETURNED from Hulett, Colby's truck was parked by the barn.

The side door opened and it seemed a dozen kids streamed out—Colby's five and four of theirs, so only nine. But close enough.

While Foster and Beau were too cool to race to their parents, Avery and Vaughn immediately bounded over.

AJ scooped Vaughn into her arms and kissed both of his cheeks. "Hey pard. Miss me?"

"Daddy!"

Cord looked down into his daughter's freckled face. "Hi punkin." He smoothed back her hair, avoiding the strands coated with glitter. "Didja have fun?"

"*So* much fun." Avery put her feet on the tops of Cord's boots and demanded to be danced around while detailing every minute of their time at Aunt Keely's.

Colby waved as he loaded up his crew and took off.

Not thirty seconds later, Kyler pulled in, rap music blaring from the open windows of his pickup.

Foster and Beau headed that way first, followed by Avery and Vaughn.

Ky hopped out and announced, "Threw two TDs last night."

"Congrats. Did anyone tape it?"

Ky rolled his eyes. "You mean record it? Dad, no one says tape anymore."

Cord muttered, "My bad," low enough only AJ heard him.

She snickered. "Pretty sure no one says that anymore either."

They watched as Kyler loaded Vaughn—and his big backpack—into a piggyback ride and the rest of the brat pack followed him inside like ducklings.

Cord leaned over and kissed her cheek. When she turned her head, he kissed her square on the mouth. Twice.

"What was that for?"

He draped his arm over her shoulder and pulled

her close. "Because I wouldn't want you to forget I'm a pretty affectionate man."

If you enjoyed Cord and AJ's short story, continue reading for a snippet of their original story in Cowgirl Up and Ride, which is currently available in KU.

ONE

AMY JO FOSTER had loved Cord McKay her entire life.

It didn't matter he was thirteen years her senior. Or he'd once dated her older sister. Or his little sister was her best friend. She fell for him hard the day she'd fallen off her horse.

That hot, dusty afternoon teased the edges of her memory. She'd been clip-clopping along on the gravel road connecting the Foster and McKay ranches when a rattler spooked her pony and bucked her off. She'd twisted her ankle on the unexpected dismount, unable to scramble away from either the angry snake or the truck barreling toward her.

Her life flashed before her eyes.

But the tires on a big Ford dually locked up and the truck skidded to a stop. A young man jumped out, swooped in and picked her up. His work-roughed hands tenderly brushed rocks from her knees and wiped the tears from her dirty face. He carried her to the passenger side of his truck, burned rubber over the snake and drove her home, keeping hold of her hand as she sobbed.

Amy Jo had a devil of a time climbing out of his rig, not because of the injury to her ankle, but mostly because she hadn't *wanted* to get out. She remembered sitting in that truck cab, surrounded by the scent of horses, of chewing tobacco, of hay, dust and the underlying tangy aroma of his cologne, and she'd wanted to stay right there with him forever.

With his dark good looks, bold smile and gentle ways, Cord had become her ideal, her dream, her savior, her prince charming in battered cowboy boots and a sweat-stained white Stetson.

No man had ever held a candle to him.

She'd been a whopping five years old at the time.

So, Amy Jo secretly worshipped Cord McKay throughout the years. Even after he moved to Seattle. Even after he returned to Wyoming married to a floozy from the West Coast. Even after the woman birthed a son. Even after the idiot abandoned Cord and their baby Ky.

She'd especially loved Cord then because she'd ached to pick up the pieces of his broken life. To make him whole. To crack the bitter shell he'd erected around his heart. To show him real, everlasting love was worth waiting for. In her core, her heart, her very soul, Amy Jo knew she was meant to be that one special woman.

Problem was she hadn't been a woman at the time either; she'd been a shy eighteen-year-old girl.

Too young.

The other problem was Cord hadn't seen her beyond the clumsy blonde pig-tailed friend of his little sister. Or as a family acquaintance with a neighboring ranch. Or recently as his son's babysitter.

That'd been the worst kind of torture. Being in Cord's house. Hearing Ky rambling from sunup to sundown about his father. Seeing Cord's unmade bed—one side rumpled, one side pristine. His lone coffee cup in the sink. Catching a whiff of his shaving cream as she lingered in front of the same bathroom mirror he used every day.

Seemed Amy Jo spent her life waiting for her chronological age to catch up with the age of her soul. Waiting for other people to believe she was old enough to know her own mind, even when she'd made it up at the tender age of five.

Now that she was twenty-two, she could stake her claim.

Standing in front of her bedroom mirror, she adjusted her cleavage in the skin-tight shirt the color of ripe apricots. She applied a coat of shiny pink lip-gloss. Finger combed her hair and inhaled a deep breath.

In all the hours she'd fantasized about Cord McKay, he'd never really noticed her.

Come hell or high water, Amy Jo would change that tonight.

Also by Lorelei James

BLACKTOP COWBOYS® SERIES
Corralled
Saddled and Spurred
Wrangled and Tangled
One Night Rodeo
Turn and Burn
Hillbilly Rockstar
Wrapped and Strapped
Hang Tough
Racked and Stacked
Spun Out

BLACKTOP COWBOYS® NOVELLAS
1001 DARK NIGHTS
Roped In
Stripped Down
Strung Up
Tripped Out
Wound Tight

WILD WEST BOYS NOVELLAS
Mistress Christmas
Miss Firecracker

THE WANT YOU SERIES
I Want You Back
Want You to Want Me

THE NEED YOU SERIES
What You Need
Just What I Needed
All You Need
When I Need You

MASTERED SERIES
Bound
Unwound
Schooled (digital only novella)
Unraveled
Caged

STANDALONE NOVELS
Unbreak My Heart
Dirty Deeds
Running With The Devil

STANDALONE NOVELLAS
Lost In You
Wicked Garden
Ballroom Blitz